I0567554

Understanding

Kerouac's

On The Road

Understanding Kerouac's

On The Road

Edward Renehan

2012
New Street Communications, LLC
Wickford, RI

newstreetcommunications.com

© 2012
Edward Renehan

All rights reserved under International and Pan-American Copyright
Conventions. Except for brief quotations for review purposes, no part
of this book may be reproduced in any form without the permission of
New Street Communications, LLC.

Published 2012 by
New Street Communications, LLC
Wickford, Rhode Island
newstreetcommunications.com

To the loving memory of

Jane Arden ("Sparrow") Stoneback

When I die,
Hallelujah by and by,
I'll fly away.

Contents

Preface

Celebrating the fiftieth anniversary of Jack Kerouac's *On the Road* in 2007, Tony Long called the book an anthem for the "crazy ones" and noted that the novel "has spoken to every generation since it appeared, and it's still got plenty to say in a society where consumer conformity is sold as rebellion by savvy marketers and the tyranny of the pop-culture machine smothers any truly iconoclastic voice. … Kerouac himself never fit in, although he spent a good part of his life trying to. He died young and unhappy, but to measure *On the Road* against the bitterness of its author's life is to miss the point. The novel is about the yearning for freedom. What you do with that freedom once you've attained it ... well, that's up to you. It was then. It is now." Long further praised *On the Road* as a "banshee cry" against orthodoxy – against the "spiritual death" of "gray conformity." (*Wired*, August 30th, 2007.)

The occasion of the fiftieth anniversary codified and made official *On the Road*'s permanent place in the pantheon of great American classics. In this, it sits alongside such other influential, controversial and revolutionary works as Twain's *The Adventures of Huckleberry Finn*, Melville's *Moby-Dick*, Whitman's *Leaves of Grass* and Thoreau's *Walden*. To this day, the book sells tens of thousands of copies annually. Indeed, reading it has become a rite of passage for American (and, for that matter, European) youth – at least those youth who are bright and astute enough to ponder large questions: the meaning of the world around them, and their own meaning within that world – those who wish to *find themselves*, as the saying goes.

One wonders, however, how many actually *get it* and find *themselves* as opposed to the ghost of someone else. The message of Kerouac's intensely-autobiographical *On the Road* – insofar as it has any message at all – is quite simply that one should seek out and follow his or her own unique road. More to the point: One must make one's own personal pilgrimage towards one's own personal Truth. For Kerouac, Truth equaled spirituality and redemption. "The unhip story of a search for God and human goodness has eluded most readers," writes John Leland. " … the challenge for [Kerouac's] novel … was to repair a breach in post-Whitman America and find goodness within it. Like Whitman, Kerouac sang for the land and its flawed people – multitudinous like himself, filled with potential and contradiction. … The narrator's name [*Sal Paradise*] is a not-so-subtle clue to this intention: He is Salvatore and his road is to Paradise. … Sal's offering will be in revelation, aiming not to fix America's problems but to expatiate them. American man was good but fallen; he needed atonement … "

The many who come away from the novel mimicking what they perceive to have been the Beat lifestyle simply do not understand what Kerouac offers. *On the Road* was not meant to inspire readers to specifically do drugs, bed-down with strangers and travel cross-country any more than *Walden* was written to inspire readers to specifically build a house in the woods and ponder solitude. Kerouac himself loudly criticized would-be Beats whom he saw as imitators, since imitation was the direct opposite of what *On the Road* had actually been about: an *individual* spiritual quest. Also, as shall be shown, Kerouac most certainly *did not* recommend the particulars of the lives conducted by his desperate, nihilistic and sad antiheroes (including himself).

Philosophy aside, Kerouac's novel was revolutionary from a strictly literary point-of-view in that it represented something completely new in terms of execution. Its breathless voice, its rushing locomotive-like prose, its unprecedented jazz-like syncopation, had not been known before. Thus it invited (and received) scathing ridicule from the literary establishment of the late 1950's. But as time has shown, those critics be damned. As a rite of passage, as a benchmark in the development of American Letters, and as a looming influence over much prose that followed it, *On the Road* remains as relevant today as it has ever been – not as an instruction manual for life, but most certainly as a talisman of true soul-, enlightenment- and God-seeking freedom. The novel (a story of true "lost souls" seeking redemption which some find, and many not) has entered into the very DNA of America. As Bob Dylan commented: "It changed my life like it changed everyone else's."

Kerouac has in turn become a brand name: an industry unto himself. The Kerouac estate generates a small fortune annually. America's preeminent outsider – who during his lifetime expressed gross dissatisfaction in having been pigeon-holed as the *Hippie Homer* – has become a lion of the American cultural landscape, albeit a frequently misconstrued lion.

Kerouac photographed by Tom Palumbo, 1956.
Used by permission.

Beats

Jack Kerouac was born to French-Canadian working class parents in Lowell, Massachusetts, March 12, 1922. Raised in a devout Catholic environment, he was destined always to incorporate Catholic tenets and symbols into his various shifting belief systems, while always calling himself a Catholic. (This is true even of the concept *Beat*. According to biographer Ann Charters, one of Kerouac's inspirations for the term was the idea of being "Beatific," or in a state of beatitude. He equated it to St. Francis, "trying to love all life, being utterly sincere and kind and cultivating 'joy of heart.'" In other words, St. Francis was Beat.) Per Leland: Kerouac "drifted away [from Catholicism] in his teens and as an adult discovered and eventually discarded Buddhism, settling finally on a home-grown form of mystic Catholicism. But he held always to the mysterious and gnostic, and to a prophet's sense of time, which articulates the past within the fallen present."

An older brother, 9-year-old Gerard (whose memory would later inspire the novel *Visions of Gerard*), died of rheumatic fever when Jack was four.

Kerouac spoke a French-Canadian version of French before he spoke English, beginning to pick up the latter language only around the time his brother died. He eventually would write some poetry in French, and even launched the initial writing of *On the Road* in that language. (Two novels by Kerouac, written completely in French, remain unpublished.)

A football star at Lowell High School, Kerouac entered Columbia University on a football scholarship. Soon thereafter, a cracked tibia and a general disinterest in the grind of formal college academics led him to drop-out. He also failed, in rapid succession, to adapt to both the Merchant Marine (1942) and the U.S. Navy (1943). Kerouac rebelled against the conformist natures of life within each service. His career in the Navy lasted a total of nine days, ending with a medical discharge after a diagnosis of schizoid personality from a military psychiatrist.

He wrote his first novel in 1942, a piece based on his Merchant Marine experiences entitled *The Sea Is My Brother*. The book did not see print until 2011. Kerouac himself thought the novel apprentice-work and inadequate, and never endeavored to get the book published in his lifetime. It was during this same period that Kerouac came to know the circle of writerly friends ultimately to be known as the Beats, among them William S. Burroughs (*Old Bull Lee* in *On the Road*), Allen Ginsberg (*Carlo Marx*), Lucien Carr (*Damion*), Neal Cassady (*Dean Moriarity*), John Clellon Holmes (*Tom Snark*) – whose 1952 book *Go* is widely considered to be the first Beat novel – and Herbert Huncke (*Elmer Hassel*), the latter a confirmed career criminal and, like Burroughs, a heroin addict.

Kerouac's first published novel, *The Town and The City*, received respectable reviews when brought out by Harcourt Brace in 1950, but did not sell well. People who return to this novel today find a very different voice from what they know as that of *On the Road* and subsequent works. Kerouac had yet to develop the wildly-flowing,

Bebop-inspired prose style for which he would become famous. The measured cadences of *The Town and the City* are reminiscent of such early influences as Thomas Wolfe. Nevertheless, like all of Kerouac's prose, the text is quite autobiographical. The town, in this instance, is a facsimile of Kerouac's native Lowell, while the city is New York, populated by the early Beats Kerouac found there. Ginsberg, Carr, Burroughs, Huncke and others all make appearances under various pseudonyms.

Harcourt editor Robert Giroux – who picked up the novel on the recommendation of Columbia's Mark Van Doren, one of Kerouac's former professors – sliced 400 pages out of Kerouac's massive manuscript before sending the book to press, and carefully oversaw Kerouac's work in rewriting key sections. Giroux later refused to purchase *On the Road* and rejected all Kerouac manuscripts subsequently offered him.

*

As early as 1948, Kerouac wrote a friend that he was meditating an "American picaresque," tentatively titled *On the Road,* which would deal with "hitch-hiking and the sorrows, hardships, adventures, sweats and labors of … two boys going to California, one for his girl, the other one for Golden Hollywood or some such illusion, and having to work in carnivals, lunch-carts, factories, farms, all the way over, arriving in California finally where there is nothing … and returning again." Elsewhere he commented that *On the Road* "was really a story about two Catholic buddies roaming the country in search of God. And we found him. I found him in the sky, in Market Street San Francisco (those 2 visions), and Dean (Neal) had God sweating out of his forehead all the way. THERE IS NO OTHER WAY OUT FOR THE HOLY MAN: HE MUST SWEAT FOR GOD. And once he has found Him, the Godhood of God is forever Established and really must not be spoken about."

Two Catholic boys.

Neal Cassady – Kerouac's (*Sal Paradise's*) iconoclastic partner, mentor and corrupter *Dean Moriarity* in *On the Road* – was most certainly Kerouac's closest friend among the Beats. Four years younger than Kerouac, Cassady had spent much of his youth living on skid-row in Denver with his alcoholic father – that is, when not in reform schools. (Cassady's mother died when he was a very young boy.) From age 13 he routinely engaged in such petty crimes as stealing cars and shoplifting. At the same time, he possessed a great, untrained intelligence. At age 15 he encountered high school teacher Justin Brierly, who mentored him, introduced him to great literature, encouraged him to write and, apparently, gave him his first homosexual experiences.

Upon being released from an 11-month prison term in 1945, Cassady married a 15 year old acquaintance, LuAnne Henderson (*Marylou* in *On the Road*), and moved to Manhattan at the urging of another veteran of Brierly's tutoring, Hal Chase (*Chad King* in *On the Road*) who was then active in the Columbia-based circle of writers in which Kerouac moved.

A flagrant philanderer, Cassady practiced both heterosexuality and homosexuality, sometimes engaging in menage-a-trios evenings with Ginsberg and Henderson.

Carolyn and Neal Cassady photographed by Kerouac, 1951.
Used by Permission.

Cassady's sexual relationship with Ginsberg was to
continue for two more decades although the two men,
usually separated by vast chunks of geography, often did
not see each other for many months at a time and took
many other lovers.

Cassady separated from LuAnne after just a few months of marriage, and had the union annulled. A couple of years later, in 1948, he married Carolyn Robinson (*Camille* in *On the Road*), by whom he was to father three children. Not long after their marriage, the couple moved to Monte Sereno, a suburb some 50 miles south of San Francisco, and Neal took a job as brakeman on the Southern Pacific Railroad. Among the storms that would define this marriage was Cassady's additional [bigamous] 1950 marriage to Diane Hanson (*Inez* in *On the Road*), by whom he fathered a son.

Somewhat miraculously, Carolyn stayed with Neal and did not divorce him until 1963. Less than a year after the publication of *On the Road*, Neal was arrested for possession of marijuana and served two years in San Quentin. Cassady, already a legend in underground circles as the model for Dean Moriarity, was to be made even more of a cultural icon when portrayed vividly in Tom Wolfe's *The Electric Kool-Aid Acid Test* as the main driver and penultimate "Merry Prankster" of Ken Kesey's bus *Furthur* in the now-legendary road-trip of 1964. Wolfe's book was published 1968, the year of Cassady's overdose death in Mexico.

*

Throughout the late 1940s, Cassady and Kerouac (sometimes joined by others) made the several drug-enhanced cross-country road trips which would eventually fuel the creation of *On the Road.*

Both drugs and promiscuity (including the homosexual promiscuity of Carlo Marx, aka Ginsberg) loom large throughout the journeys of *On the Road* – journeys geographical, spiritual and metaphorical.

As documented by Gerald Nicosia in his study of Kerouac entitled *Memory Babe*, Jack was clearly – like Cassady and Burroughs – bisexual, albeit a confused and unhappy bisexual. In fact, he seems to have been genuinely ashamed of the homosexual side of his nature. Depending on to whom he was speaking, and how drunk or high he was, he would manifest his old football player machismo and routinely refer in derogatory terms to "fags" and "queers."

Not long after a night of sex with Gore Vidal (a night documented in Vidal's *Palimpsest*), Kerouac ridiculed Vidal in a letter to Malcolm Cowley as "a pretentious little fag." Even in *On the Road* itself, Kerouac uses language which evidences a fundamental disdain for gays. ("The car belonged to a tall, thin fag who was on his way home to Kansas and wore dark glasses and drove with extreme care; the car was what Dean called a 'fag Plymouth'; it had no pickup and no real power. 'Effeminate car!' whispered Dean in my ear.") Several years after Jack's death, Allen Ginsberg told Barry Gifford and Lawrence Lee that Kerouac always "avoided" dealing with the memories of "his own homosexual encounters … "

As if to compensate for his homosexual urges, Kerouac frequently (and often drunkenly) bragged about the many women he had bedded, at one point estimating (probably without exaggeration) that he had slept with more than 250 during the late forties.

Kerouac told his friend Connie Murphy that his initial exposure to homosexual practices had been in the Merchant Marine during long voyages with no women available. He explained to Murphy that the homosexuality of his crew-mates was not his "cup of tea," but that he had been "thirsty" and thus drank. Truth be told, Kerouac – although far more active with women than with men – enjoyed numerous homosexual encounters on dry land.

Among his heterosexual affairs was one he carried on with Carolyn Cassady while at the same time deflecting Neal's repeated pleas for a menage-a-trios. Kerouac himself was married three times. He also fathered a daughter, Jan, whom he barely knew and at first disclaimed. Kerouac's character in *On the Road*, Sal Paradise, is strictly heterosexual, while the bisexuality of Neal (Dean) is alluded to only once, and then quite casually.

Throughout the novel, Kerouac is nowhere near as reticent in discussing his characters' use of substances. The very phrase *on the road* was derived from one of Neal Cassady's euphemisms for being high on drugs. Cassady constantly indulged in a range of illicit pharmaceuticals, often to excess, as did Burroughs and nearly all the other Beats. As has been previously noted, Burroughs was addicted to heroin. At one point he dealt the drug in Greenwich Village in order to support his habit.

Kerouac first tried marijuana and the powerful amphetamine Benzedrine in 1940, while frequenting Harlem jazz clubs. The Benzedrine often caused him to hallucinate and allowed him to stay awake for days on end. Later on, in 1952, the surrealist poet Philip Lamantia introduced Kerouac and Cassady to the wonders of peyote. For the San Francisco-born Sicilian-Catholic Lamantia "drug taking was a sacrament," writes Nicosia, "a form of Communion ..." Kerouac concurred. He said the peyote allowed him a powerful revelation of how it must feel to die. He did not find the experience unpleasant.

Burroughs, in turn, introduced Jack to the pleasures of morphine and hashish. Kerouac also adopted the use of mescaline which, Nicosia reports, inspired "an immensely reassuring vision of the world as 'One Flower,' with everyone united peacefully in a constellation of saints whose flashing dance it was his [Kerouac's] duty to report

… " (Three years after the publication of *On the Road*, Kerouac would partake of LSD and, along with Allen Ginsberg, also be introduced to psilocybin by none other than the man himself: Timothy Leary.)

In life and in his novel, Kerouac (as inspired by Lamantia) rationalized drug-taking as a legitimate exercise in God-seeking – a tool of liberation. Per Nicosia, Jack believed that in this "evil world"

> … *the Light of the spirit was often hidden by darkness and had to be sought out. Once the Light was found, however, it would "not be a defense against this world but an entryway into the next"; and, ironically, that world was habitable not by men, but only by ghosts. Hence Jack found "no hope in this world for any of us except temporary glimpses of the Light and the transient bliss of such moments."*

The inhabitants of *On the Road*, like the Beats themselves, seek transient bliss in the thrill of racing cars down midnight highways, in drugs, in liquor, in random sex and in the riffs of untethered jazz.

This latter item cannot be emphasized enough. The wildly dissonant experiments of Thelonious Monk, along with the soaring Bebop of Charlie Parker ("Bird") and Coleman Hawkins, translated to Kerouac and his friends as perhaps the purest of art forms – so very spontaneous that its greatest moments endured for just one orgasmic climax before falling up, like cinders, to heaven, never to be heard again. In this the wafting sounds of jazz mirrored the luminescent, brief moments of bliss avidly sought and exalted in by that tangled lot of self-destructive misfits called the *Beats*.

Dean and I went to see [George] Shearing at Birdland in the midst of a long, mad weekend. ... Shearing began to rock; a smile broke over his ecstatic face; he began to rock in the piano seat, back and forth, slowly at first, then the beat went up, and he began rocking fast ... his combed hair dissolved, he began to sweat. ... Dean was sweating. "There he is!

That's him! Old God! Old God Shearing. Yes! Yes! Yes!" ... Shearing rose from the piano, dripping with sweat; these were his great 1949 days before he became cool and commercial. When he was gone Dean pointed to the empty piano seat. "God's empty chair," he said. ... God was gone; it was the silence of his departure. ... Dean was popeyed with awe. This madness would lead nowhere. I didn't know what was happening to me, and I suddenly realized it was only the tea that we were smoking; Dean had bought some in New York. It made me think that everything was about to arrive – the moment when you know all and everything is decided forever.

Revelation

In 2001, Indianapolis Colts owner Jim Isray paid $2.43 million at auction to purchase Kerouac's original manuscript for *On the Road* – the famous scroll upon which he'd rendered his self-described "spontaneous" draft of the novel. The seller was the estate of Kerouac's recently-deceased brother-in-law, Anthony Sampas. Many were outraged at the scroll's falling into private hands. "Some scholars and curators," wrote the *Chicago Tribune's* Noan Schoenberg, "say that such an important literary holding should, ideally, be in the hands of a public institution, such as a major library. Among their concerns: the scroll, which was typed on cheap pieces of paper attached to each other by means of paste and tape, is fragile. It is also of immense value to scholars, who have not yet performed comprehensive studies of the hand-written corrections that dot the manuscript. Another potentially fruitful area of study is the difference between the scroll and the finished book ..." Carolyn Cassady, in turn, called the selling of the scroll a "blasphemy."

In retrospect, however, it is hard to complain. Isray commissioned extensive (and expensive) restoration by experts at Indiana University's Libby Library. In 2004, he made the scroll available for a three-year tour of institutions across the United States, this culminating on the fiftieth anniversary of the book's publication. Additionally, Isray routinely makes the scroll available to qualified scholars. In these days of libraries – especially scholarly libraries – being reined in by increasingly draconian budget cuts, such private collectors as Isray should be welcomed. 2007 saw publication of the original scroll manuscript.

*

Less than a year before the writing of *On the Road*, Kerouac and Cassady - "a holy con man with a shining mind" – transacted their last major road-trip together. The two traveled from Denver down into Mexico, driving a dilapidated '37 Ford, doing drugs and bedding women at a frantic pace. Per Tom Clark:

As Neal idled the Ford through villages, Jack gazed
out the window in ecstasy at "hillbillies, paisanos, cats
of the pampas, campo people." This was the universal
"fellaheen" of which Spengler had spoken – it was the
"Indian thing." In one village where they stopped to
buy marijuana and women, Jack experienced what he
later called his greatest "vision" of Neal – "the one
great occasion when I saw ... everything not only
about him but America, all of America as it has been
conceptualized in my brain." They smoked a "great
rugged cigar" of pot, and as Neal drove slowly
through dusty streets in search of a local whorehouse,
Jack suddenly saw his friend glow "like a sun" and
become "all rosy as a rosy balloon and beautiful as
Franklin Delano Roosevelt." [At the same time,
Kerouac] began to envision himself as the "Great
Walking Saint of On the Road*," a pilgrim who would*
walk cross an otherwise doomed America to pay for its
sins – perhaps in the final moments of history.

*

Prior to his outpouring of *On the Road* onto the scroll, Kerouac had in fact fiddled around with several drafts and approaches over the course of several years, attacking the story from a range of narrative angles, including that of a young black boy who spoke in the first-person. (This experiment was subsequently published after Jack's death as the short novel *Pic*.)

Returning to New York after his final quest with Neal, Kerouac slowly began to codify the vision that would represent the core of the *On the Road* we know today, especially in the way of narrative voice. Kerouac was later to credit Cassady with inspiring the frenetic, breathless prose which came to define not just *On the Road*, but the bulk of Kerouac's writing thereafter. He said he took much of his minimalist, fast-paced "confessional" style from "seeing how good old Neal Cassady wrote his letters to me, all first person, fast, mad, confessional, completely serious, all detailed, with real names."

Tom Clark:

Cassady's letters had begun to provide Kerouac with valuable stimulus and example. They were profane, awkward, oddly inspiring. Cassady said that when writing, he felt "like Proust ... Remembrance of your life and your eyeball view are actually the only two immediate first hand things your mind can carry instantly." Neal's letters, containing his own "eyeball view," were heavily autobiographical. Indeed, he told Jack that, contrary to the prevailing literary style of the time ("to create fiction"), everything he said should be taken "as straight case-history."

Cassady's mad, rushing, unadorned prose represented nothing so much as it represented *speed* – a frantic, nonstop, consciously-unrefined eruption of scenes, dialogue and images. In other words: raw, visceral and ill-considered *Truth*. No doubt Benzedrine and coffee helped Cassady's prose flow in this way, just as the same items would help Kerouac's.

Kerouac wrote the full first draft of *On the Road* in the small New York apartment of his then-wife, Joan Haverty, who – though breaking up with him – nevertheless grudgingly, allowed him this place to work and write. (The address: 454 West 20th Street. Despite their estrangement, Joan emerged from the period of writing pregnant with Kerouac's daughter Jan.)

On April 2nd, 1951, Kerouac assembled the many sheets of paper that were to make-up his scroll and taped them together. He told a friend that he was a 100-word-a-minute typist, and that stopping to put new paper into the typewriter interrupted his train of thought. That problem solved, he began to write: one long paragraph, single-spaced. He played music as he wrote. Dennis McNally: "Kerouac had written *The Town and the City* to Jascha Heifetz; *On the Road* was set to the flying pound of Max Roach's Bop drums, the whole of the book bursting with energy, with a feeling of life struggling inside a deathly society, energy burning bright before the laws of entropy …"

Biographer Paul Maher: "Ten days into his typing, Jack told his friend Ed White that an estimated 86,000 words had been written thus far. Kerouac was exhilarated that it was going so smoothly. … By April 22, Kerouac had completed a 125,000 word novel. Rejuvenated and thrilled, he explained to Cassady that the work was about 'you and me and the road.' Ginsberg, who had read from the work in progress and had seen that Kerouac had used real names in lieu of pseudonyms, told Cassady that the 'hero is you.'" Kerouac relayed to another friend how he had found the writing of *On the Road* to be a mystical experience. The prose seemed not to have been composed, but gifted from a source unknown. Thus it was also inviolate, like a Bible text.

Years later, Bob Giroux would recall a disheveled Kerouac showing up at his office carrying a roll of "rubbery sheets, like Thermo-fax paper … teletype sheets pasted together." Kerouac unraveled the 100-foot scroll across Giroux's floor. According to Giroux, Jack pontifically announced: "I don't make any corrections. That's the way it will be." Harcourt's rejection of Jack's book, and his ultimatum, was not only assured but nearly immediate.

*

Kerouac revered Melville, especially the latter's *Moby-Dick*. In the original draft of *On the Road*, Sal Paradise calls himself "a veritable Ishmael." As was the case with that itinerant sailor, Paradise must travel to restore his soul. And like Ishmael with Ahab, Paradise meets his captain and corrupter in Dean Moriarity. (Note: Just like Melville, Kerouac was to die disheartened, believing that his best work had been misunderstood.)

Not long before writing the scroll draft, Kerouac spent several days reading an edition of Melville's *Pierre* edited and with an introduction by Harvard psychologist Henry Murray. In Kerouac's copy of the book, we find these words of Murray's underlined: "Melville was not writing autobiography in the usual sense but, from first to last, the autobiography of his self-image." So too did Kerouac write of his self-image, rather than of himself. Of all the characters in *On the Road*, Sal Paradise is the least similar to his original. Paradise – like Ishmael – is to some extent an uninitiated innocent participating in a novitiate from which he will emerge fundamentally changed. In other words, Paradise is not – like Kerouac – a cynical ex-merchant-sailor and frequenter of jazz clubs and drug dens. He is not, like Kerouac, a man quite well-versed in the ways and corruptions of the world.

Paradise's many experiences at the side of Dean Moriarity are a revelation, and nothing less. The revelations and ecstasies he finds in his heightened, most extreme moments with Dean and others (the rambling priesthood of the Beats) are ones he never quite realized he was searching for, until he discovers them. Like saints and prophets before him, he walks his road on a quest to know the unknowable.

Second Religiousness

Six years ensued between the original composition of *On The Road* and its final 1957 publication by Viking Press. During this period, Kerouac spent much time as a lone voyager. He moved about the country by hitchhiking and hopping freights, often camping out or else bunking with friends (at one point in the Mill Valley, California cabin of poet Gary Snyder, another time in Randall Jarrell's Washington D.C. basement). He took up a solitary job as a fire lookout on Desolation Ridge, in the Sierras (where he wrote prose that would later become a part of *Desolation Angels),* worked with Neal Cassady as a brakeman on railroads, and lived with William S. Burroughs in Mexico and Algiers. (While crashing in the New York apartment of Helen Parker, he met Woody Guthrie's protege Ramblin' Jack Elliott. After Jack treated Kerouac to a selection of Woody's best songs, Kerouac reciprocated by reading the whole of *On the Road* aloud over the course of three nights.)

Amid these years he also wrote several more novels –
among them *The Subterraneans* (composed during three
Benzedrine-driven evenings), *Doctor Sax* and *Visions of
Cody* – all of which remained unpublished after being
turned down by several houses, including New Directions.
On the Road, in turn, was rejected by a host of publishers
after Harcourt (Ballantine, Farrar/Straus and,
initially,Viking), with Allen Ginsberg often acting as go-
between for Kerouac in approaching those houses. (A
number of these works were meant by Kerouac to be parts
of a cycle of autobiographical novels he referred to as *The
Duluoz Legend*.)

Ginsberg was himself, at first, frankly skeptical about
On the Road.

In a letter dated June 12th, 1952, Ginsberg praised but
also criticized the novel. "The language is great," he told
Kerouac, "the blowing is great, the inventions have full-
blown ecstatic style." At the same time, however, he said:
"I don't see how it will ever be published … I don't know if
it would make sense to any publisher – by make sense I
mean, if you could follow what happened to what

characters where. … Where you are writing steadily and well, the sketches, the exposition, it's the best that is written in America, I do believe. … but on my mind I am worried by the whole book. It's crazy (not merely inspired crazy) but unrelated crazy … crazy in a bad way, and *got* aesthetically and publishing-wise, to be pulled back together, reconstructed. I can't see anyone, New Directions, Europe, putting it out as it is. They won't, they won't. … *On the Road* just drags itself over the goal line of meaning to someone else (or to me who knows the story); it's salvageable. I mean it needs to be salvaged."

Kerouac answered Ginsberg's heartfelt honesty with an abusive letter dated October 8th. "And you who I thought was my friend – you sit there and look me in the eye and tell me [*On the Road*] is 'imperfect' as though anything you ever did or anybody was perfect? … Do you think I don't realize how jealous you are and how you … would give your right arm to be able to write like the writing in *On the Road*?" He ended by wishing death on Ginsberg and several other friends who'd offered criticism of the work. Ginsberg knew his friend well, and was used to his

Benzedrine- and alcohol-fueled tirades. He refused to respond in kind, and instead wrote offering a more optimistic assessment of another Kerouac manuscript: *Doctor Sax*. The rift mended, and Ginsberg – despite his misgivings with regard to *On the Road* – did his best to help Kerouac find homes for both novels.

Writing to Ginsberg from New York in June of 1954, Kerouac reported: "*On the Road*, which I retitled *Beat Generation* so I could sell it, was just turned down by Seymour Lawrence at Atlantic Monthly-Little Brown with the same little tune about 'craftsmanship' ... Book is now at E.P. Dutton's ... All the others are in my agent's drawers unread and dusting – what the hell's the use?" (Kerouac had recently acquired representation by Stanley Corbert of the firm Sterling Lord.) Thankfully, the title *Beat Generation* did not stick.

When Kerouac asked one of his heroes, William Carlos Williams, to write a recommendation of the book for presentation to Random House, Williams declined. Kerouac had almost given up by the time Ginsberg managed to interest the great Malcolm Cowley, then at Viking.

Cowley:

My first notice of Kerouac was the submission of On the Road *to the Viking Press, and specifically to me at the Viking Press. I don't remember how it came in. Allen Ginsberg may have brought it. It had, by that time, passed through several stages. At some stage it was revised and retyped so that when it came into the Viking Press it was a conventional paged manuscript. I read it with great interest and enthusiasm, and I told a Viking [editorial] meeting about it and got a few more readings for it, but no, they wouldn't publish. I thought: "Here is something new. Here is something that ought to get to people. A way has to be prepared for it." Viking was a rather conservative house, and they thought this was too much out of the beaten path for our salesmen to place in the bookstores, so the manuscript stayed on my desk. Kerouac came to see me several times, and I said: "What you will have to*

do first is get some of this published in magazines." So
I excerpted the section called "The Mexican Girl" and
gave it to the Paris Review, *which accepted it with*
some enthusiasm. Then I looked for what other section
could stand by itself. It was the one on jazz in San
Francisco, and Arabelle Porter took that for New
World Writing.

It in fact took several years for Cowley to finally
convince his editorial board Kerouac's book was worth
taking a risk on.

Once a deal was finally done, Viking editors Rae
Everett and Helen K. Taylor worked closely with Kerouac
to extensively revise *On the Road* before publication. In
contemplating Kerouac's work, Taylor made it plain to the
author that she believed "large chunk-cutting" was
necessary to make the narrative move faster, though not to
remove the many obscenities, which she had no problem
with. (On the other hand, Viking's attorneys – concerned
about libel – insisted that Kerouac concoct fictional names
for the real-people he'd used as models for characters,

down to the use of their actual names. Thus William S. Burroughs became *Old Bull Lee*, Neal Cassady morphed into *Dean Moriarity*, Allen Ginsberg grew into *Carlo Marx*, Kerouac himself became *Sal Paradise*, and so forth. As double-assurance, despite the name changes, the lawyers made Kerouac get signed libel-releases from all those whose thinly-veiled personas he'd written into his story.)

A generation was to later claim the book as a road-map to a gloriously free and creative life, but Taylor considered it something else altogether. "There is no redemption for these psychopaths and hopeless neurotics, but they don't want any." The novel, she said, exposed the "raw sociology" of the "hipster generation." And she did not consider that sociology to be pretty.

She believed that the book itself, however, breathed with a vivid freshness. Taylor noted Kerouac's "bold writing talent" which she described as both "lavish" and "reckless ... it is almost as if the author did not seem to exist as an outside agency of creation." Another Viking editor, Evelyn Levine, saw the book as chronicling another

"Lost Generation," but one which instead of going to Paris stayed "right here," journeying the country to try and discover themselves. She called Kerouac a "fresh, new (and fascinating) talent – a jived-up Walt Whitman." Still, Levine agreed with Taylor that the manuscript needed a great deal of work, adding that the female characters were crudely drawn and underdeveloped, "almost none of them … real." (For whatever reason, Kerouac was always to fail in his attempts to render women realistically.)

Although the guru of "spontaneous prose" would later claim otherwise, Kerouac worked hard at the revisions asked for by Cowley and Taylor. "Jack did something that he would never admit to later," Cowley recalled. "He did a good deal of revision, and it was very good revision. Oh, he would never, never admit to that, because it was his feeling that the stuff ought to come out like toothpaste from a tube and not be changed, and that every word that passed from his typewriter was holy. On the contrary he revised, and revised well." Shortly before publication, Kerouac even went so far as to suggest a highly market-oriented, and utterly inartistic, revision to the title. "It occurred to me," he told Sterling Lord, "maybe it would double sales to change the title to *Rock and Roll Road* or at least to invent a similar subtitle."

An internal memorandum at Viking delivered an absurdly simplistic synopsis of *On the Road* for the education of sales reps:

> *This is a narrative of life among the wild bohemians of what Kerouac was the first to call "the beat generation." It carries us from New York to Denver, from Denver to San Francisco, then back to New York (with a detour through the Mexican settlements of the Central Valley) – then New York, New Orleans, San Francisco, Denver again, Chicago in seventeen hours in a borrowed Cadillac, Detroit, New York, Denver once more, and a Mexican town – the characters are always on wheels. They buy cars and wreck them, steal cars and leave them standing in fields, undertake to drive cars from one city to another, sharing the gas; then for variety they go hitch-hiking or sometimes ride a bus. In cities they go on wild parties or sit in joints*

listening to hot trumpets. They seem a little like machines themselves, machines gone haywire, always wound to the last pitch, always nervously moving, drinking, making love, with hardly any emotions except a determination to say "Yes" to any new experience. The writing at its best is deeply felt, and extremely moving. Again at its best this book is a celebration of the American scene in the manner of a latter-day Wolfe or Sandburg. The story itself has a steady, fast, unflagging movement that carries the reader along with it, always into new towns and madder adventures, and with only one tender interlude ... It is real, honest, fascinating, everything for kicks, the voice of a new age.

A new age? Kerouac himself considered his novel to be more of an obituary than a birth announcement. Just weeks before the book's release, Viking publicist Patricia MacManus asked Kerouac to write an essay in which he might formally define the "Beat Generation," this to be placed by MacManus in some appropriate publication on or near the date for the book's debut. In the essay, Kerouac declared that Beat as a movement outside the culture had virtually disappeared by 1950, and was now years away from having been relevant. It was, in fact, an historical artifact.

Kerouac explained that he had drawn his initial inspiration for the Beat idea from philosopher Oswald Spengler who, in *Decline of the West*, articulated the idea of a "Second Religiousness." According to Spengler, the inevitable cycle of civilizations always led back to the rise of "primitive religion, which had receded before the grand forms of the early faith." This primitive religion would return "to the foreground, powerful, in the guise of the popular syncretism that is to be found in every culture at this phase." (For those without a dictionary handy, *syncretism* is the combining of different [often seemingly contradictory] beliefs, particularly religious beliefs – finding peace between the practices of various schools of thought, and refusing to accept or respect traditional boundaries. In all, it represents a new and revolutionary way of seeing.)

Per Spengler, the "Second Religiousness" appears "in all civilizations as soon as they have fully formed themselves as such and are beginning to pass, slowly and imperceptibly, into the non-historical state ... " According to Kerouac, it was what Spengler called the "first, genuine, young religiousness" – which he declared to be the vital prelude to the "Second Religiousness" – that the Beats sought so desperately. And now that they'd paved the way, the "Second Religiousness" had entered the culture.

Kerouac had witnessed what he believed to be the "first, genuine young religiousness" throughout the late 1940s. It manifested in "strange talk we'd heard among the early hipsters of 'the end of the world' at the 'second coming,' of 'stoned-out visions' and even visitations, all believing, all inspired and fervent and free of Bourgeois-Bohemian Materialism." Kerouac contended that by 1957, the types who populated *On the Road* had "vanished into jails and madhouses, or were shamed into silent conformity; the generation itself was short-lived and small in number." And their job was done.

Writing to Cowley, Kerouac said of the essay: "It's the only statement I ever made about the Beat Generation, and that is the only statement about it ever made by the originator of the idea … though my article may seem deceptively light-headed it really is the score." But Kerouac's interpretation did not fit the script the world would write for him. Per biographer Paul Maher Jr.: "Although Kerouac determined that the word 'Beat' was no longer relevant, it wouldn't be long before America redefined and distorted its meaning. If Kerouac's characters were no longer Beat, the media would reinvent the term in a way that in time would stigmatize his life and art."

In interviews related to the publication of the book, Kerouac (a frequently stoned and/or drunk Kerouac) would try again and again to express the complexity and importance of the Beat philosophy as he'd envisioned it, never with success. Reporters – most of them hostile – did not want to hear it. Consider this comment penned by journalist Maurice Dolbier after interviewing the author: "... When one's mind [begins] to boggle at the vision of Presley's side-burns and John-Paul Sartre and bop-talk and rock-'n'-roll and Brando on a motorcycle as units of a religious revival, you are reminded of the posthumous revival of James Dean and the trance-visions induced by drugs and young wonder. Mr. Kerouac hammers out the case with anonymous instances of strange manifestations, foreshadowings of the end of the world and the Second Coming, hipsters who have seen angels and devils, and reports quite casually that he too has heard the heavenly music while speeding along a California highway." (*NY Herald Tribune*, September 22nd, 1957.)

A few months later, quite weary of trying to make people understand, Kerouac tried to put the question to bed by telling interviewer Mike Wallace "Beat" was basically nothing, just an "old phrase" that he'd "knocked off one day and they made a big fuss about." (*New York Post*, January 28th, 1958.)

Stigmata

On the Road hit bookstores on September 5th, 1957 and sold so well that Viking ordered a second printing fifteen days later. The novel was destined to sit on the *New York Times* bestseller list for a full five weeks.

Critics greeted *On The Road* with either great praise or great detraction – polar extremes, with no middle ground.

Gilbert Millstein's review in the *New York Times*, published September 5th, would prove to be the one and only unreservedly positive reaction Kerouac ever got from that newspaper. (Kerouac, newly arrived in New York, bought the midnight edition of the *Times* as soon as it was available, and read it with relief while sitting with his friend and sometime-lover Joyce Glassman in the Donnelly Bar on Columbus Avenue.)

Millstein praised the novel as being nothing short of a milestone. "[The publication of *On the Road* is an] historic occasion ... [This novel] is the most beautifully executed, the clearest and the most important utterance yet made by the generation Kerouac himself named years ago as 'Beat,' and whose principal avatar he is ..." Millstein compared *On The Road* to Hemingway's *The Sun Also Rises*, in that the former book was certainly to become the "testament" of the Beat Generation, just as Hemingway's novel had served the same purpose for his own "Lost Generation." But there, Millstein insisted, all similarity ended. "Technically and philosophically, Hemingway and Kerouac are, at least, a depression and a world war apart."

Millstein continued:

... The "Beat Generation" and its artists display readily recognizable stigmata. Outwardly, these may be summed up as the frenzied pursuit of every possible sensory impression, an extreme exacerbation of the nerves, a constant outraging of the body. (One gets "kicks"; one "digs" everything, whether it be drink, drugs, sexual promiscuity, driving at high speeds or absorbing Zen Buddhism.) ... Inwardly, these excesses are manic to serve a spiritual purpose, the purpose of an affirmation still unfocused, still to be defined, unsystematic. ... The "Beat Generation" was born

disillusioned: it takes for granted the imminence of war, the barrenness of politics and the hostility of the rest of society. It is not even impressed by (although it never pretends to scorn) material well-being (as distinguished from materialism). It does not know what refuge it is seeking, but it is seeking.

Twenty-nine years down the road, in 1986, the *Los Angeles Times* would specifically cite Millstein as the critic who "propelled both Kerouac and his Beat Generation beatitudes from limbo to limelight."

It is perhaps worth noting here the great mercurial randomness of the book review process. A reviewer with a profoundly conservative philosophy when it came to literature, Charles Poore, had originally been intended to review the work for the *Times*. However, for an unknown reason, the assignment wound up being given instead to Millstein. Poore would have most certainly condemned Kerouac's novel as less than worthless.

Millstein was so enthusiastic about *On the Road* that he hosted a party to celebrate Kerouac and his book, a party which Kerouac – bemused by countless demands for interviews and appearances – refused to attend.

Millstein's appraisal had appeared in a daily edition. Not much later, the *New York Times Sunday Book Review* offered mixed praise in a brief review – "In Pursuit of 'Kicks'" – by freelance writer David Dempsey.

Thirty years ago it was fashionable for the young and the weary – creatures of Hemingway and F. Scott Fitzgerald – simply to be 'lost.' Today, one depression and two wars later, in order to remain uncommitted one must at least flirt with depravity. On the Road *belongs to the new Bohemianism in American fiction in which an experimental style is combined with eccentric characters and a morally neutral point of view. It is not so much a novel as a long affectionate lark inspired by the so-called 'Beat' generation, and an example of the degree to which some of the most original work being done in this country has come to depend upon the bizarre and the offbeat for its creative stimulus. Jack Kerouac has written an enormously readable and entertaining book but one reads it in the same mood that he might visit a sideshow – the freaks are fascinating although they are hardly part of our lives.*

Dempsey added that this was a road, "as far as the characters are concerned, that leads nowhere – and which the novelist cannot afford to travel more than once."

A number of other reviewers proved even less generous.

Writing in the *Atlantic Monthly* (October), Phoebe Lou Adams (in a piece entitled "Ladder to Nirvana") praised Kerouac's "distinctive … readable" style, but said the novel "constantly promises a revelation or a conclusion of real importance and general applicability, and cannot deliver any such conclusion because Dean is more convincing as an eccentric than as a representative of any segment of humanity." Overall, Adams condemned *On the Road*'s "severe simplicity."

In the *Nation* (November 16th), Herbert Gold (a Columbia classmate) criticized not just Kerouac's novel, but the entire philosophy and lifestyle it represented.

The hipster-writer is a perennial perverse bar mitzvah boy, proudly announcing: 'Today I am a madman. Now give me the fountain pen.' The frozen thugs gathered west of Sheridan Square or in the hopped-up cars do not bother with talk. That's why they say 'man' to everybody – they can't remember anybody's name. But Ginsberg and Kerouac are frantic. They care too much, and they care aloud. 'I'm hungry, I'm starving, let's eat right now!' That they care mostly for themselves is a sign of adolescence, but at least they care for something, and it's a beginning. The hipster is past caring. He is the criminal with no motivation in hunger, the delinquent with no zest, the gang follower with no love of the gang; i.e., the worker without ambition or pleasure in work, the youngster with undescended passions, the organization man with sloanwilsonian gregorypeckerism in his cold, cold heart.

Apparently believing Kerouac's hype about the novel being the result of an organic eruption of prose, Truman Capote famously quipped: "That's not writing, it's typing." (Capote's put-down came two years after the novel's publication and was spoken on the talk-show *Open End.*) Prominent critic Carlos Baker said he was left "sad and blank" by the "busy travelogue" of Kerouac's novel. In a review entitled "Flings of the Frantic," *Newsweek* insisted "the only thing that prevents *On the Road* from careening headlong off into the trash heap is the sheer impetus of novelist Kerouac's fast-tempoed, bop-beat prose." (*Newsweek*, September 9th.) *Time* (September 9th) criticized Kerouac's "Whitmanesque weakness for cataloging nearly every experience" and dismissed his novel as nothing more than an attempt to "create a rationale for the fevered young who twitch around the nation's jukeboxes and brawl pointlessly in the midnight streets." The headline for Thomas Curley's *Commonweal* review (September) made clear his point of view: "Everything Moves, But Nothing is Alive."

Revolutionary art – in this case an entirely disruptive revolution in prose-style, storytelling and the very notion of what constitutes *story* – is always hard to understand. It is also disturbing and, for the most part, unwelcome. The established order never likes a revolution. And with regard to *On the Road*, the literary establishment played its role perfectly.

Notably, just about every review, whether positive or negative, failed to acknowledge Kerouac's vision of the work as the narrative of a journey toward spiritual enlightenment: a holy pilgrimage by flawed mortals seeking some semblance of Truth.

Purgatory

Kerouac died in October 1969, just two months after the Woostock Festival. Thus he lived long enough to understand how a fundamentally nihilistic generation had come to impose its own interpretation on him and his work. As early as 1960 he wrote: "Realized last night how truly sick and tired I am of being a 'writer' and 'Beat' – it's not me at all – yet everybody keeps hammering it into me. … They're going to INSIST that I fit their preconceived notion of the 'Beatnik Captain,' as tho I was some degenerate bearded insurrectionist." He said he believed the "beatnik movement" was little more than "a big move-in from intellectual dissident wrecks of all kinds and now even Anti-American, America-haters of all kinds with placards who call themselves *beatniks*."

From the very start of his relationship with the group he'd dubbed the *Beats*, Kerouac had seen himself as separate from them: a tag-along and observer. For example he always disapproved and was offended by Burroughs, Ginsberg and others actively cultivating relationships with members of the criminal underworld, who they tended to view not as societal nuisances, but rather as the ultimate "individuals" governed only by their own laws, principles, beliefs (or lack of same). As well, he was different from them in his (admittedly tidal and individualistic, but nevertheless quite sincere) Catholic faith.

As John Leland explains in *Why Kerouac Matters*: "It should be noted that Sal is not one of the mad ones. ... He keeps a writer's distance, shambling behind 'as I've been doing all my life after people who interest me.' ... As a narrator he is a silent fly on the wall, writing the action as if he were reading ... letting Dean drive."

The same goes for we readers. "We are not really mad ones either," says Leland. And we would not want to be. We are, with Kerouac, watchers at a spectacle. "However romantic the adventures look on the page, most readers wouldn't want to live like that. The small core of friends who formed the Beat generation was shaped by suicide, depression, psychosis, institutionalization, addiction, alcoholism, jail and early death." Leland reminds us that Burroughs shot and killed his wife, Lucien Carr knifed and killed a man who pursued him with unwanted sexual advances, and at least three of the group wound up as suicides. Additionally Burroughs, Ginsberg, Huncke and Vicki Russell (Fairy Godmother to the group's discovery of Benzedrine) did "time," as of course did Cassady.

In a 1968 *Washington Post* essay entitled "After Me, The Deluge," Kerouac rejected the notion that he was "the great white father and intellectual forebear who spawned a deluge of alienated radicals." He was instead the "intellectual forebear of modern spontaneous prose."

He said he had no politics. He was an artist – an artist equally as unhappy with the Counter-Culture as he was with the Establishment – a man in the middle. While the Establishment was characterized by "political lust and concupiscence, a ninny's bray of melody backed by a ghastly neurological drone of money-glut," the Left, "though quite understandably alienated nay disgusted by the scene," offered "no better plan [to] the grief-stricken citizens but fund-raising dinners of their own." The rebelling students, meanwhile, were barbarians, acid-heads and parasites who did not "believe in the written word ..."

The Vietnam War was an evil tragedy, but so too was the destruction of the Columbia campus. This fallen, temporal world was imperfect and always would be. Only fools thought it fine as is, and only fools thought it fixable. Neither the status quo nor its alternatives mattered a whit. Jack saw the future in the past; both were a shambles. The only possible redemption was individual, and lay within.

An unredeemed Cassady had died not long before – fearful, desolate, and completely broken by his antihero fame. "I get in a group," he told his ex-wife Carolyn, "and everyone just stares at me, expecting me to perform … and my nerves are so shot, I get high … and there I go again. I don't know what else to do." Neal fled to Mexico in January of '68 to avoid several California traffic warrants. He died there on February 4th from an apparently unintentional overdose of alcohol combined with Seconal, collapsing beside some railroad tracks where he'd been walking, alone.

Seventeen years earlier, Neal had predicted his death at a young age, either from cancer caused by incessant masturbation or from being overworked on a chain gang after being sent to prison for the rape of a teenager. Cassady's actual end was nearly as dark.

*

At an autumn 1968 taping of Bill Buckley's *Firing Line,* a soddenly drunk Kerouac joined several others in expounding on the topic of "The Hippies." Kerouac's distaste for one fellow panelist, East Village poet and wanna-be Beat Ed Sanders (publisher of *Fuck You/A Magazine of the Arts* and co-founder of the Fugs), was palpable, but then so too was his distaste for Buckley.

Riding up the elevator with Sanders, who peppered his hero with questions, Kerouac growled: "Get the fuck off my back, kid." During the taping, Kerouac (rather randomly) attacked Lawrence Ferlinghetti, whom he appears at the moment to have blamed for turning his original beautiful Beat ideal into "the Beat mutiny, the Beat insurrection, words I never use, being a Catholic."

Throughout the conversation, the already-wasted Kerouac sipped whiskey out of a coffee cup. When Sanders alluded to Kerouac being part of a literary movement with Allen Ginsberg, Kerouac loudly disclaimed his alliance with Ginsberg or any movement *per se*. "I'm not connected with Ginsberg, and don't you put my name next to his." As he spoke, the cameras panned to a long-haired Ginsberg sitting in the audience – there because he'd accompanied his friend Kerouac at the latter's urgent, last-minute request.

Ginsberg held no grudges, and Kerouac probably forgot his statement a few seconds after he uttered it. McNally: "Paying no mind to his old friend's confused hostility, Allen bade Jack farewell on the street corner outside, touched him tenderly, and said with a smile, 'Goodbye, drunken ghost.' Allen never saw him alive again."

Long after Kerouac's death, Burroughs discounted his old friend's claimed disassociation from the Beats and – even more importantly – from his central role in inspiring what became the youth rebellion of the sixties. It did not matter what Jack's intentions were, said Burroughs. The fact was that a generation had adopted his book as their own, and took from it what they would. Such, he insisted, was the nature of art. The artist creates; the viewer interprets. And in the long run, the latter always outranks the former.

*

"I'm not a beatnik; I'm a Catholic," Kerouac told an interviewer one month before his death. Then he pointed to a portrait of Pope Paul VI hanging on the wall of his modest Florida home. "You know who painted that? Me."

When Kerouac died at age 46 (from complications of prolonged alcoholism), a score of literary eulogists rose to praise him. Writing in the *New York Times*, Joseph Lelyveld celebrated Kerouac as a "hero to youth" who had "rejected middle class values." Lelyveld quoted Ginsberg as calling Kerouac "a very unique cat – a French Canadian Hinayana Buddhist Beat Catholic savant." Others extolled Kerouac as a rebel, a philosophical leader, a guru and a torch-bearer for his self-defined "mad ones." They all said, unanimously, that *On the Road* stood as his greatest testament.

The man who lay in a Lowell funeral home wearing a checkered black and white jacket and a red bow-tie, rosary beads placed carefully in his overlaid hands, would probably have disagreed with all these assessments save for the last. But then, he was not consulted.

First Edition, 1957.

Bibliography

Charters, Ann. *Kerouac: A Biography*. 1973.

Clark, Tom. *Jack Kerouac: A Biography*. 1984.

Gifford, Barry and Lawrence Lee. *Jack's Book: An Oral Biography of Jack Kerouac*. 1978.

Kerouac, Jack. *On the Road*. 1957.

Leland, John. *Why Kerouac Matters*. 2007.

Melville, Herman. *Pierre*. (Edited with an Introduction by Henry Murray.) 1949.

McNally, Dennis. *Desolate Angel: Jack Kerouac, The Beat Generation, and America*. 1979.

Morgan, Bill and David Stanford (Editors). *Jack Kerouac, Allen Ginsberg: The Letters*. 2010.

Nicosia, Gerald. *Memory Babe: A Critical Biography of Jack Kerouac*. 1983.

About the Author

Edward Renehan serves as managing director of New Street Communications, LLC, the publisher of this book. He has previously authored some 18 books for such houses as Oxford University Press, Basic Books/Perseus, Crown, Doubleday and McGraw-Hill, and has held major positions with a number of Manhattan-based publishing firms, most prominently serving seven years as Director of Computer Publishing Programs for Macmillan (later Newbridge, a Division of K-III, now known as PriMedia). Renehan has as well served as a consultant to the publications division of the United States Holocaust Memorial Museum, and other publishing organizations. He lives near Newport, Rhode Island.

About the Publisher

Founded June of 2010, New Street Communications, LLC publishes first-quality nonfiction in a range of fields (also, through Dark Hall Press, first-quality original horror and science fiction). New Street's nonfiction interests include the intersection of digital technology and society; transformative business communication and innovation (particularly the conceptualizing of elegant new tools, markets, products and paradigms); environmental issues; socially-relevant children's literature; travel; and literary criticism. We are located in the historic seaport town of Wickford, RI, near Newport.

 *newstreetcommunications.com*

Also from New Street ...

Beast: A Slightly Irreverent Tale About Cancer (and Other Assorted Anecdotes) by James Capuano

Charles Dickens and the Making of A CHRISTMAS CAROL by Michael Norris

Computing: A Business History by Lars Nielsen

Elements of the Novel by Eileen Charbonneau

Hemingway's Paris: Our Paris? by H.R. Stoneback

Teaching Salinger's NINE STORIES by Brad McDuffie

www.ingramcontent.com/pod-product-compliance
Lightning Source LLC
Chambersburg PA
CBHW070353130626
46556CB00007B/3153